First published in the United States, Great Britain, Canada,
Australia, and New Zealand in 2003 by North-South Books,
an imprint of Nord-Süd Verlag AG, Gossau Zürich, Switzerland.

Distributed in the United States by North-South Books Inc., New York.

Library of Congress Cataloging-in-Publication Data is available.
A CIP catalogue record for this book is available from The British Library.
ISBN 0-7358-1517-8 (trade edition)   10 9 8 7 6 5 4 3 2 1
ISBN 0-7358-1518-6 (library edition)   10 9 8 7 6 5 4 3 2 1
Printed in Belgium

For more information about our books, and the authors and artists
who create them, visit our web site: www.northsouth.com

A Michael Neugebauer Book
North-South Books
New York / London

Good Bread
A Book of Thanks

Brigitte Weninger

Anne Möller

My mother and I baked bread together.
It smelled so delicious!
It tasted good too!

The bread was made from many
different grains of wheat.

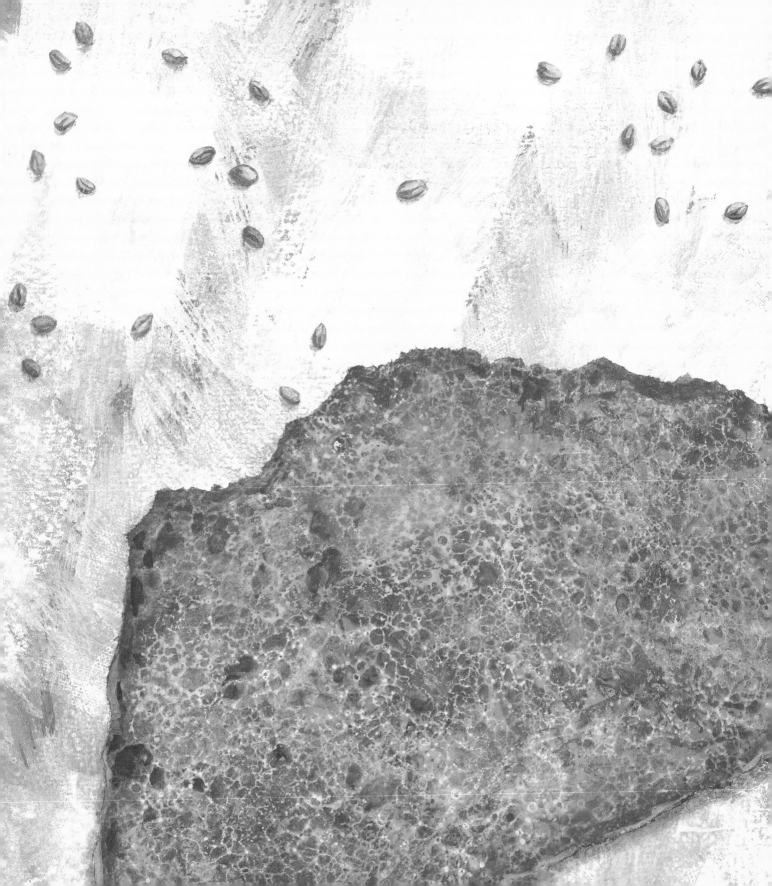

In the spring, farmers sow grains
of wheat in the damp earth.

The grains grow roots and shoots.
Every day they grow bigger.

By summer, each shoot has developed a head.

In autumn, when the wheat turns from green to brown, it is ripe. Farmers cut the wheat and thresh it, which separates the kernels from the rest of the plant.

Every head contains from 30 to 65 kernels of grain.
From one grain, so many have grown!

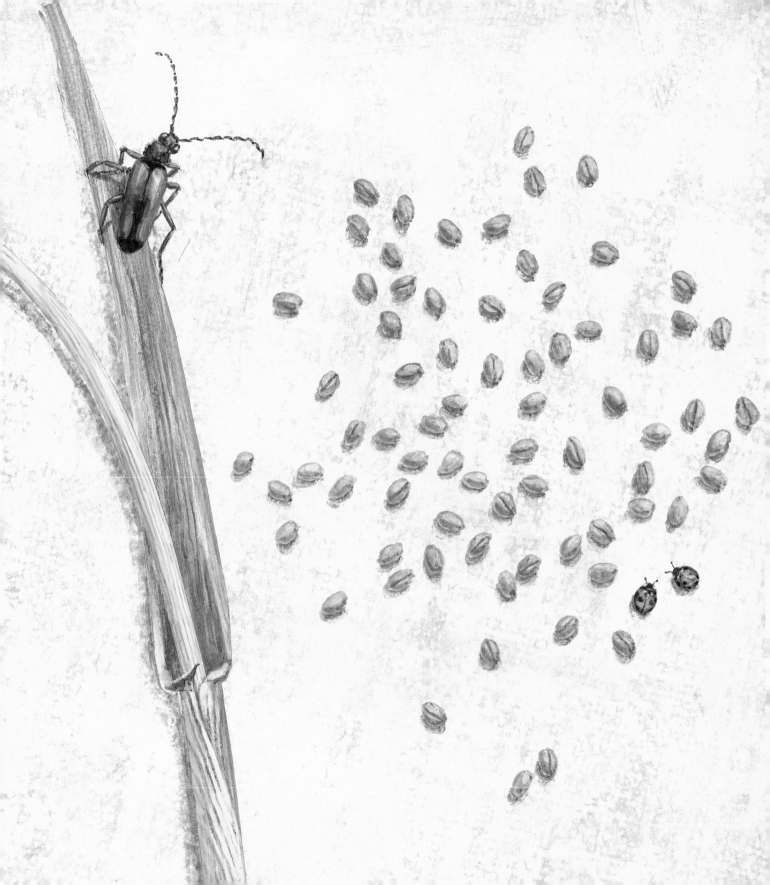

My mother and I grind the grains of wheat
in a hand mill to make flour.

Then we knead the flour with salt, water, yeast, and seasoning to make dough.

We shape the dough into a big loaf
and I put it into the oven to bake.

I hope that other children have bread like this to eat.

I am so thankful for this good bread.